P9-BIC-804

OLIVIA
and the Fancy Party

by Cordelia Evans
illustrated by Shane L. Johnson

Simon Spotlight
New York   London   Toronto   Sydney   New Delhi

Based on the TV series OLIVIA™ as seen on Nickelodeon™

SIMON SPOTLIGHT
An imprint of Simon & Schuster Children's Publishing Division
1230 Avenue of the Americas, New York, New York 10020
OLIVIA™ Ian Falconer Ink Unlimited, Inc. and © 2014 Ian Falconer and Classic Media, LLC
All rights reserved, including the right of reproduction in whole or in part in any form.
SIMON SPOTLIGHT and colophon are registered trademarks of Simon & Schuster, Inc.
For information about special discounts for bulk purchases, please contact Simon & Schuster Special Sales
at 1-866-506-1949 or business@simonandschuster.com.
Manufactured in the United States of America 0614 LAK
First Edition 1 2 3 4 5 6 7 8 9 10
ISBN 978-1-4814-0364-1
ISBN 978-1-4814-0365-8 (eBook)

Mother shuffled through a stack of mail as she and Olivia walked through the front door. She pulled out a bright pink envelope and handed it to Olivia. "Looks like this is for you, Olivia."

Olivia opened the envelope as quickly as she could without ripping it. "It's an invitation to a party at Francine's house!" she exclaimed.

"How nice of Francine to invite you to her party!" said Olivia's mom. "You'll have to remember to use your best manners!"

Olivia imagined a party at Francine's house would be very fancy. Francine and
all her guests would be dressed in their finest clothes, and waiters in tuxedos
would walk around, carrying fancy foods on silver platters.

But I've never been to a fancy party before, thought Olivia. She imagined herself spilling a glass of juice all over Francine's party dress.

Olivia shuddered as she tried to get the image of a shocked Francine covered in grape juice out of her head.

"You're right, Mom," she said. "I'm going to practice all week, and by the time the party comes around, I'll be the perfect guest!"

Up in her room, Olivia got out the *Big Book of Manners* her grandma had given her. "Let's see . . . the perfect party guest should greet her host politely, have good posture, practice proper table manners, and, of course, have appropriate attire! I know just what to wear."

Olivia went to her closet and pulled out her new party dress. It was pink with a big bow. She couldn't wait to wear it to Francine's party!

All week Olivia practiced being a good party guest. Whenever anyone came to the door, she worked on being polite and making conversation.

"Thank you *ever* so much for stopping by," she told Julian.

"What?" Julian said, confused. "You asked me to come over, remember?"

"You look fabulous today—blue is definitely your color," Olivia said to the mailman.
"Wow, thanks!" responded the mailman. "Um, could you please sign for this package?"

Next, Olivia looked up proper table etiquette in her *Big Book of Manners*. She demonstrated for William as she set the dinner table.

"You have to start from the outside and work your way toward your plate," Olivia explained. "So, you use the first, outermost fork to eat your salad and the first spoon to eat your soup, and then you use the next round of utensils to eat your main course."

William cooed.

"And always remember to put your napkin in your lap before you start eating,"
Olivia said. She placed a napkin in William's lap.
He looked at her and threw it on the floor.
Olivia sighed.

Then Olivia decided to work on her posture. Her *Big Book of Manners* said it was rude to slouch at the dinner table.

She closed the book, placed it carefully on her head, and began to walk slowly around her room, standing up very straight.

"What are you doing, Olivia?" asked Ian as he walked past her room.

"My book says that this will help me sit up straight and be more balanced," she answered. "Do you want to try?"

Ian placed a book on his head and tried to follow her. Right away, the book fell off.

"It's okay. Try again!" said Olivia encouragingly.

Again, the book fell off as soon as Ian took a step.

"I guess I'm not very balanced," he said.

Finally, the day of the party arrived. Olivia came down the stairs wearing her fancy pink dress.

"I'm ready," she declared.

"Is that what you're wearing to the party?" asked Olivia's mom.

"Of course!" said Olivia. "A guest should always look her best."

"Okay," said Mother. "But it's only noon. The party isn't for another three hours."

Exactly three hours later, Olivia walked up to Francine's front door, prepared to greet her hostess politely. She was about to knock when she noticed a colorful sign on the door: PARTY GUESTS: PLEASE COME AROUND BACK!

Hmm, thought Olivia. She walked around to the backyard, carefully holding up her skirt. The sound of people talking and laughing got louder and louder as she approached. When she peeked around the corner, she was surprised to find that the party was . . .

Party Guests
please come
around back!

. . . a cookout! There were tables covered in red-checkered tablecloths and piled high with food. All around, adults and kids were chatting and snacking, and Francine's dad was over by the grill wearing a big white apron.

"I guess this party isn't as fancy as I thought," said Olivia. She looked for Francine, and spotted her along with the rest of their friends. They were running around throwing water balloons at each other!

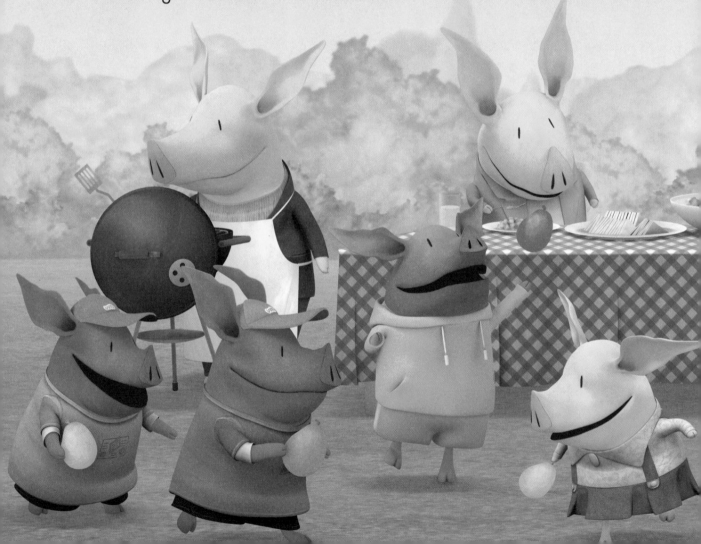

Francine ran up to Olivia and was about to throw a big, bursting balloon at her when she noticed her outfit.

"Wow, what a pretty dress, Olivia!" exclaimed Francine. "I guess you probably don't want to get it wet."

Olivia thought for a minute. "Well, the most important part of being a good guest is participating in the activities your hostess has planned." She picked up a water balloon and tossed it in the air a few times. "So, I guess I'm getting wet . . . if you can catch me!"

And she threw the water balloon at Francine and ran away laughing.

Even though the party wasn't fancy, Olivia still managed to use her manners. After the water balloon fight there was an egg race. Each person had to balance an egg on a spoon and walk from one end of the yard to the other. The first person to make it to the finish line won.

"And the winner is . . . Olivia!" declared Francine's mom as Olivia crossed the finish line ahead of everyone else. All her work balancing the book on her head had paid off!

Dinner was a buffet, so there were no place settings, but Olivia gathered all her utensils from the baskets on the table and set them up as she had practiced. "Wow, that looks so fancy, Olivia!" said Daisy. "Can you show me how to do that?" Soon all of Olivia's friends had proper place settings and were picking up their outermost forks to eat their salads.

When the party was over, Olivia's mom came to take her home.

"Thank you for having me," Olivia told Francine's mother.

"You're very welcome," said Francine's mother. Then, to Olivia's mom, she said,

"Olivia was the most well-mannered guest at the party—and the

best-dressed, too!" Olivia beamed.

"What are you doing, sweetie?" asked Mother later that evening as she came into Olivia's room to say good night.

"I'm writing a thank-you note to Francine and her family," Olivia replied. "A good guest always sends a note to say thank you."

"I'm so proud of you," Mother said. "Good night, Olivia."

"Good night, Mom!" said Olivia.